D1301167

The Seed Who Was Afraid to Be Planted

Anthony DeStefano

Illustrated by Erwin Madrid

SOPHIA INSTITUTE PRESS
Manchester, NH

SOPHIA
INSTITUTE PRESS

Text Copyright © 2019 by Anthony DeStefano
Images Copyright © 2019 by Erwin Madrid

Printed in the United States of America.

Sophia Institute Press®
Box 5284, Manchester, NH 03108
1-800-888-9344

www.SophiaInstitute.com
Sophia Institute Press® is a registered trademark of Sophia Institute.

No part of this book may be reproduced, stored in a retrieval system, or transmitted in any form, or by any means, electronic, mechanical, photocopying, or otherwise, without the prior written permission of the publisher, except by a reviewer, who may quote brief passages in a review.

Library of Congress Control Number: 2019947198

This book is dedicated to my
beautiful wife, Jordan.

– Anthony DeStefano

There once was a seed
who lived in a drawer,
in a room of a mansion,
by a beautiful shore.

The drawer was filled up
with seeds of all kinds,
for bushes and trees
and flowering vines.

The seed was quite happy
and had lots to do.
The drawer was quite pretty
and painted bright blue.

Cozy and warm,
the seed felt secure.
The drawer was a playground,
of this he was sure.

But all was not well.
The seed was afraid
that he would be taken
and planted one day.

The mansion, you see,
was owned by a man
whose hobby was gardening
and tending his land.

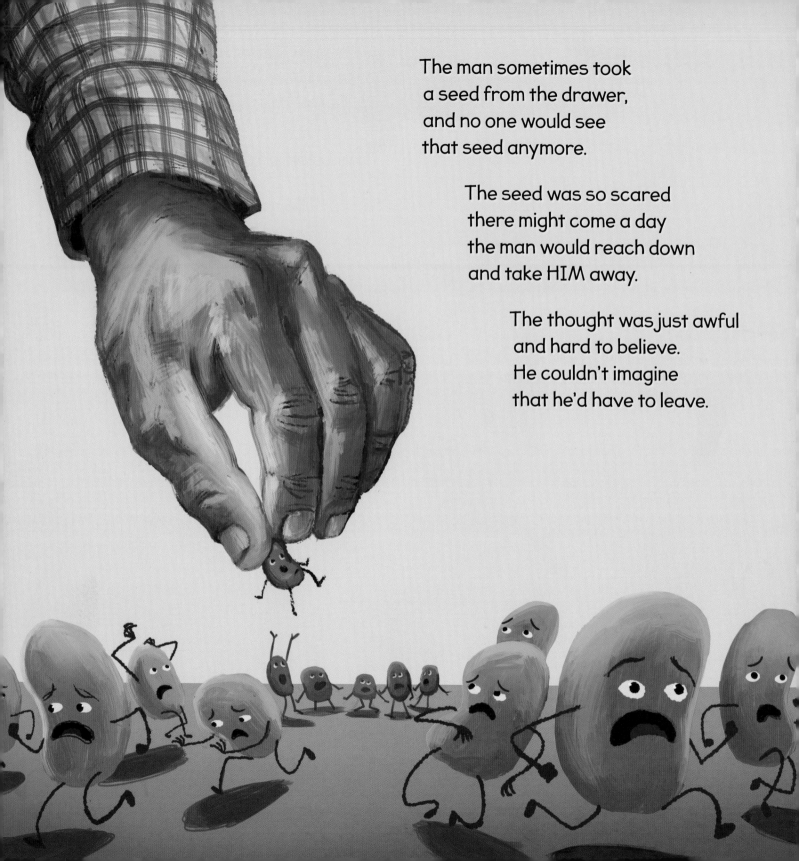

The man sometimes took
a seed from the drawer,
and no one would see
that seed anymore.

The seed was so scared
there might come a day
the man would reach down
and take HIM away.

The thought was just awful
and hard to believe.
He couldn't imagine
that he'd have to leave.

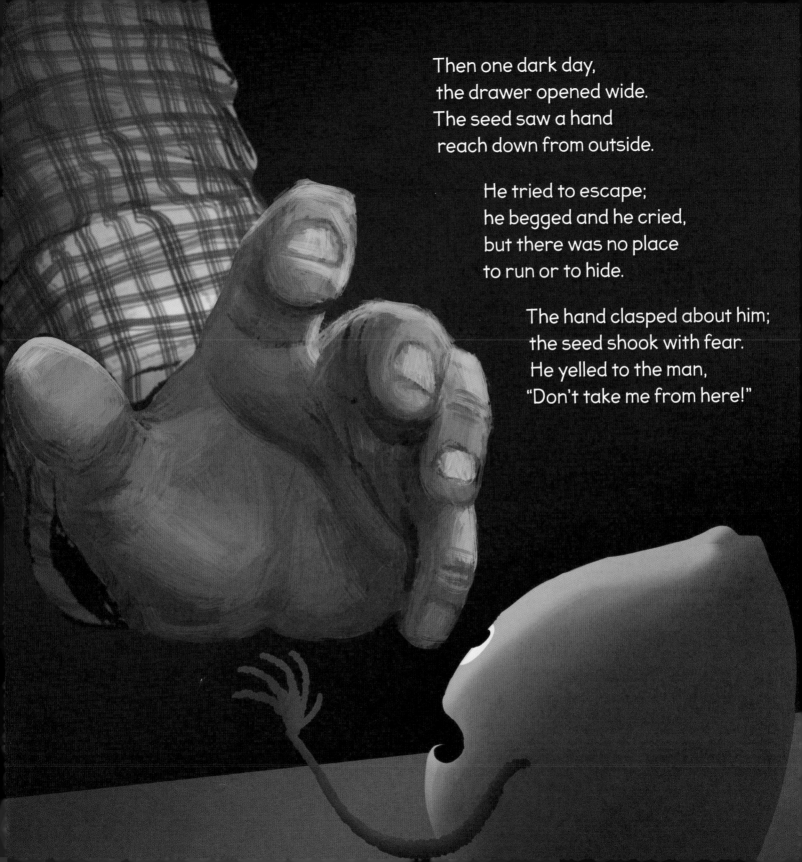

Then one dark day,
the drawer opened wide.
The seed saw a hand
reach down from outside.

He tried to escape;
he begged and he cried,
but there was no place
to run or to hide.

The hand clasped about him;
the seed shook with fear.
He yelled to the man,
"Don't take me from here!"

Outside in the garden,
the seed looked around.
He saw to his horror
a hole in the ground.

"A hole in the ground!
Oh no, it can't be!
I want to go back to my drawer,
can't you see?"

"I'm scared to be planted.
I want to be free.
I'm in so much pain
and such agony!"

The man was just silent;
he made not a sound.
He just smiled softly
and put the seed down.

The sky was deep purple.
The seed said a prayer.
The man stood above him
and buried him there.

He started to moan.
He started to groan.
He felt so abandoned,
forsaken, alone.

Tired and frightened,
he started to weep
but soon closed his eyes
and fell fast asleep.

All covered with dirt,
he dreamed he would die,
but then all at once—
in the blink of an eye—

Something took place
there in that hole,
to the seed's weary body
and terrified soul.

He started to change.
He started to glow.
The little seed stretched
and started to grow!

"What can be happening?"
the little seed cried.
"What is this feeling
I have deep inside?"

His body expanded.
He swelled and he grew.
He rose in the dirt
till his head wiggled through.

Once through the soil,
he saw a great light.
The sun in the sky
was dazzlingly bright.

Slowly but surely,
the seed was aware
of rising and climbing
up into the air.

At last the seed realized,
at last he could see,
he was really and truly
becoming a tree!

Higher and higher
the little tree went.
Into the heavens
he made his ascent.

Suddenly branches
sprang from his side.
Hundreds and hundreds
of leaves multiplied.

The branches grew nuts
and fruits that hung down.
They swayed in the breeze
and covered the ground.

Then filling the air
with fragrant perfumes,
the tree sprouted flowers
and blossoms and blooms.

Then birds began building
nests for their young,
joyfully flapping their wings
as they sung.

In the tree's branches,
the baby birds napped,
while woodpeckers pecked
at his bark full of sap.

Cardinals and blue jays
flew from above.
They played with the eagles
and owls and doves.

Squirrels and rabbits
began to appear.
Beautiful butterflies
came flying near.

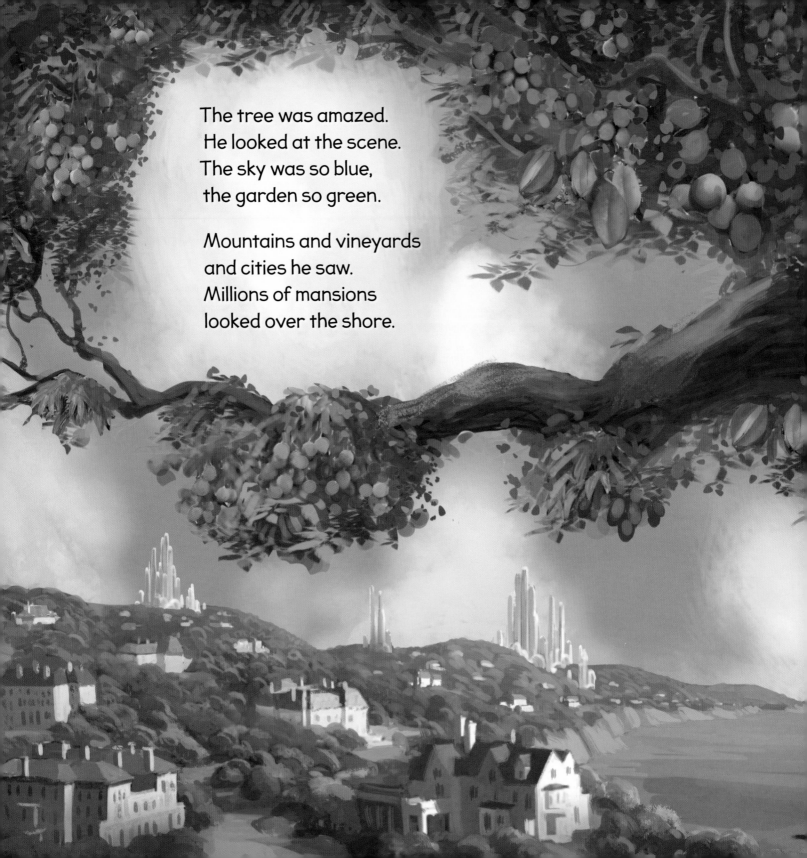

The tree was amazed.
He looked at the scene.
The sky was so blue,
the garden so green.

Mountains and vineyards
and cities he saw.
Millions of mansions
looked over the shore.

The tree was so thankful
and heavy with fruit,
he bowed to the man
in humble salute.

The man stood below,
a smile on his face.
His children were running
all over the place.

They climbed up the tree.
They swung from his vines.
They seemed to be having
 the happiest time.

The garden was sunlit.
The tree was aware
of laughter and music
and life everywhere —

Life in the garden,
life on the shore,
so much more life
than he had in the drawer.

A breeze stirred his leaves.
A wind howled through.
The tree understood
that all things were new.

The tree understood
that he had been freed.
He barely remembered
when he was a seed.

He barely remembered
his life in the drawer.
His fears disappeared
and returned ... nevermore.

The End

From the Bible

"Out of the ground the LORD God made grow every tree that was delightful to look at and good for food, with the tree of life in the middle of the garden."

– Genesis 2:9 (NABRE)

"Truly, truly, I say to you, unless a grain of wheat falls into the earth and dies, it remains alone; but if it dies, it bears much fruit."

– John 12:24 (RSV)

"The kingdom of heaven is like a mustard seed, which a man took and planted in his field. Though it is the smallest of all seeds, yet when it grows, it is the largest of garden plants and becomes a tree, so that the birds come and perch in its branches."

– Matthew 13:31–32 (NIV)

"Then Jesus went with his disciples to a place called Gethsemane… and he began to be sorrowful and troubled.… He fell with his face to the ground and prayed, 'My Father, if it is possible, may this cup be taken from me. Yet not as I will, but as you will.'"

– Matthew 26:36–39 (NIV)